FLAMINGOBOY

KINDNESS IS A SUPERPOWER

WRITTEN BY PHILLIP BOYD
ILLUSTRATED BY REECE MINGARD

For my real superheroes, my children.

I love you, forever.
PB

Written by Phillip Boyd
Illustrated by Reece Mingard
Text and Illustration Copyright © 2021 Phillip Boyd
ISBN: 9798491245406

FLAMINGOBOY

KINDNESS IS A SUPERPOWER

Not all heroes fly in the sky or leap from building to building or run faster than the speed of light.

The real heroes are the ones who dare to be themselves. The ones who inspire others to be themselves. They are kind, gentle and caring. They walk amongst us but sometimes we can't see them.

Not because they are invisible but because they are five years old and only 97 centimetres tall.

The real heroes do not even know they are heroes.
George did not know he was a hero,
until the day he became one...

George was five years old and only 97 centimetres tall when he first discovered the colour pink and from that moment on he was the boy who loved pink.

Everything pink. Pink pigs, pink fruit,
pink flowers and huge pink ice cream towers.

Then one day his mummy brought something home that would change his life forever.
A pink flamingo cuddly toy.

George, the boy who loved pink, loved his pink flamingo so much. Soon he had flamingo jumpers, bed lights and blankets and his favourite pink flamingo pyjamas and slippers.

He would dream of being a pink flamingo
and using his amazing imagination would fly
around the world having great adventures.

Racing dragons, diving with sharks and flying so
fast he would make pink lightning sparks.

The boy who loved pink was about to start school and he was nervous. His mummy told him, "Just be you."

Miss Readman asked him to say something about himself. "I'm George, I love pink and I love being a pink flamingo when I play."

Some of the children laughed. One said, "You can't be a pink flamingo, you're a boy!"

George replied, "I can be anything I want to be. At playtime I'll be racing a dragon and having a picnic on the moon." More laughter followed. George felt sad.

At home that night George felt something inside his chest. A feeling so strong that it seemed to tell him something.

It told him that he COULD be anything he wanted to be. George and his mummy had work to do.

The next day at school the boy who loved pink was nowhere to be seen. He wasn't at home. He wasn't at work with mummy. A little boy who was five years old and only 97 centimetres tall arrived at the classroom. Miss Readman turned and said, "And who are you today?"

"I'm Flamingoboy!
And I'm here to show everyone
that they can be anything they want to be."

The children were silent.
The children were smiling.
The children found this all so very exciting.

"A real superhero here in our school!" one cried.
Smiling, the teacher welcomed Flamingoboy into the class.

Playtime came at last.
Flamingoboy flew into the playground and
the children followed screaming with delight.

Flamingoboy told them,
"You can be anything you want to be.
All you need is your imagination and you'll see!"

One by one Flamingoboy saw the children changing.

A giant gorilla,

a squiggly squid,

a ballet dancer and an alien with a third eyelid.

A smiling crocodile,
a fairy frog,
a hedgehog princess and a
blue and pink striped dog.

A cuddly snowman,
a flying snail,
a sparkly starfish
and a kangaroo
with a spotty red tail.

Flamingoboy and his friends all raced the dragon, dived with the sharks and hopped on rainbow beams to a magical park.

And just as he promised they stopped for a snack,
having a picnic on the moon's bright white back.
It was a playtime they would never forget!

At that moment the ballet dancer held Flamingoboy's hand and softly said, "I'm sorry for laughing at you. I didn't mean to be mean.
I love dancing but was too scared to be seen."

Flamingoboy accepted the apology and bravely declared, "Always be yourself no matter what others think. That is what heroes do and why my cape is pink.

No one should be left out or made to feel low.
We all need love for our characters to grow.

Treat people kindly and get to know them. The reward will be a friendship that is forever and totally awesome!"

So it was not laser eyes or super strength
that gave George his finest hour.

It was showing everyone that
kindness really is a superpower.

The boy who loved pink was five years old and only 97 centimetres tall when he first became a superhero.

He is kind, gentle and caring and has the most amazing imagination.

He is always himself and he inspires others to be themselves.

He loves pink.
He loves flamingos.
He is, Flamingoboy!

FLAMINGOBOY'S
PLAYGROUND RULES

We are gentle.

We are helpful.

We play well with each other.

We listen.

We are honest.

We are kind to everyone.

We are always Flamazing!

FLAMINGOBOY
WILL RETURN SOON!

Printed in Great Britain
by Amazon